Scritch, scratch!
Rub my woolly scarf!

There are lots of pumpkins, orange and plump!
My puppy helps me pick one up.

Plonk, plonk!

Pat the smooth pumpkin
I put in my basket.

Grandma bakes pumpkins
and apple treats.
She gives me yummy pies
that are warm and sweet.

Crinkle,
crinkle!

Feel the shiny pie tin that
I put in my basket.

I jump in the leaves with all of my friends!
The leaves are my favorite colors–
brown, yellow, and red.

Touch the dry leaves that I put in my basket.

Now there's one thing left to do . . . .
We give our fall basket to you!

Hooray, hooray!

Feel the smooth wicker on your fall basket.

By Alison Inches

Illustrated by Hiroe Nakata

From warm woolly scarves and plump orange pumpkins to crunchy fallen leaves and smooth wicker baskets, celebrate fall with these autumn treats that you can touch and feel.

Look for other Little Simon books at your favorite store!

LITTLE SIMON
An imprint of Simon & Schuster Children's Publishing Division
New York London Toronto Sydney
1230 Avenue of the Americas, New York, New York 10020

Book design by Aviva Shur

Manufactured in China 0518 SDI
12 11 10 9 8
ISBN: 978-1-4169-3609-1
SimonSaysKids.com
Recommended for all ages

ISBN 978-1-4169-3609-1 $[illegible].99 U.S./$8.99 Can.
50699